bratz™

ALL-NIGHT MALL PARTY!

Don't miss these Funkadelic Bratz books!

Bratz Chatz

Cloe: Angel with Attitude!

Jade: Xtreme Kool!

Keepin' It Real!
(Based on Bratz: The Video!)

Love Is In the Air!

Model Friendship

Will Work for Fashion

Yasmin: The Princess Rules!

bratz™

ALL-NIGHT MALL PARTY!

By Charles O'Connor

Grosset & Dunlap • New York

For my mother, my sister, and my aunt
—Charles

Executive Brand Editor, Charles O'Connor

Used under license by Penguin Young Readers Group.
Published by Grosset & Dunlap, a division of Penguin Young Readers Group, 345 Hudson Street, New York, New York 10014.
GROSSET & DUNLAP is a trademark of Penguin Group (USA) Inc.
Printed in the U.S.A.

Library of Congress Cataloging-in-Publication Data is available.

ISBN 0-448-43551-9 10 9 8 7 6 5 4 3 2 1

chapter one

The excited buzz in the hallway outside Mr. Duffy's classroom meant that the weekend had already started for some students. But inside, Yasmin sat and stared at the clock on the wall, waiting for the ring of the final school bell to officially free her for what was destined to be the coolest night of the year.

She had been waiting for it for months, and now it was only hours away. Tonight was the night of the big Homecoming dance. Not just another high school dance, the Homecoming dance was bigger and better than all of the rest. Everybody who was anybody would be there. It was the perfect opportunity to make a funk-alicious fashion statement that would keep the student body at Stiles High talking throughout the new year. Having put together the coolest new outfit and the grooviest retro make-up look, Yasmin just couldn't wait to step out with her friends and strut her stuff.

But the dance was only the beginning of the evening's festivities. Afterwards, Yasmin had prepared a slumber party like no other for her and her friends. It included a supermodel fashion show featuring the craziest fashion looks, a scrumptious selection of the finest baked desserts and finger foods, and the latest and greatest video movies and dance tunes to hit the stores. Best of all, since Yasmin's parents were out of town and wouldn't be back until the next morning, it meant that she and her friends could stay up all night.

As Yasmin sat daydreaming of all the fun that was ahead, the school bell finally echoed through the hallways and school yard. Without a moment's hesitation, she grabbed her books and raced out of the classroom to her locker. When she got there, her good friend Cloe was already waiting for her.

"What took you so long?" asked Cloe.

"Mr. Duffy believes in teaching till the very last minute," responded Yasmin as she turned to Cloe and smiled. "And, speaking of the last minute . . . isn't there something you would like to tell me?"

"Huh?" responded Cloe.

"Oh, I get it," said Yasmin, brushing her long brown hair. "You want Jade and Sasha to be here when you drop the news! I see how it is."

"What do you mean?" asked Cloe, completely confused.

"You won the contest, didn't you?" asked Yasmin. "You definitely deserve it. Without a doubt. This dance is gonna be so off-the-hook now."

But before Yasmin could go on, Cloe interrupted her. "I didn't win."

Yasmin could see by the look on her face that Cloe was serious. After more than a month of hard work, Cloe was not the winner of the annual *Picture Perfect!* art contest. Her art project would *not* be used as the photo backdrop display at the big Homecoming dance that night.

"Oh, man, you were robbed!" shouted Yasmin in disbelief.

"Mr. Del Rio told me that he personally liked mine

the best, but the committee chose somebody else's instead," said Cloe.

Yasmin reached out and hugged Cloe. "I'm so sorry, Angel," she said.

"Thanks," Cloe responded. "It's no big deal."

"Who needed that stupid contest, anyway? Tonight, we're gonna have fun regardless!" declared Yasmin.

"You better believe it!" said Cloe. "Let's go find Jade and Sasha and jet outta here."

"Good idea!" responded Yasmin as both girls did a quick make-up touch-up in their locker mirrors before heading out to find their friends Jade and Sasha.

■ ■ ■ ■

Across campus, Jade and Sasha sat attentively in the journalism homeroom among a small group of students. After weeks of speculation, Mr. Kelly, the honors English teacher, had called a last-minute meeting to announce the new yearbook president.

"This year, the yearbook will be bigger and better

than ever," began Mr. Kelly. "Stiles High needs a president who can handle the changing demands of inspiring not just a team, but a whole school, to produce the best-read yearbook ever. After a careful evaluation, it has come down to two individuals. But as we all know, there can be only one."

Jade and Sasha looked at each other. They knew that no matter who was chosen, there would be no hard feelings between them.

"Therefore, I have decided to select . . . Sasha . . . for head of the yearbook committee. She has consistently proven herself to be organized and is the most obvious choice for the challenge."

As the group of students burst into applause, Sasha stood up and addressed the students before her. "Thank you. With your help, I promise to make this the best yearbook ever. No doubt." The students clapped once again and Mr. Kelly then dismissed the students. Jade approached Sasha and gave her a quick high five.

"Congrats! You deserve it," said Jade to Sasha.

"Thanks, Kool Kat!" responded Sasha. "I know you

wanted to be prez, too, but I just hope you'll be there to support."

"Are you crazy? Try to keep me away!" replied Jade. "Now, let's book! We've got a lot to do tonight!"

As the girls were making their way out of the classroom, Jade suddenly stopped and turned to Mr. Kelly. "Mr. Kelly, you said that it had come down to two individuals," she said.

"Yes, I did," said Mr. Kelly.

"Oh, no you're not!" exclaimed Sasha, realizing what Jade was up to.

"Well, if you don't mind me asking, who was the runner-up?" asked Jade.

"As a matter of fact, Jade, it was you," replied Mr. Kelly.

"Aha! I knew it!" exclaimed Jade.

"I think you would've done a fine job, too, but I think Sasha has a stronger leadership sensibility and will work just a tad better under pressure."

The seriousness of Mr. Kelly's statement stopped Jade in her tracks. "Oh, I see," she said.

"But, don't worry about it. You're still on the team.

And with your artistic sensibility, you'll be a great asset!" said Mr. Kelly as he turned to leave.

"Ummm . . . thanks," said Jade, slowly making her way out of the classroom.

"Ladieeees!" yelled Cloe and Yasmin from down the hall. "Is your meeting finally over?"

"Yeah," responded Sasha.

"Well, what's the verdict?" asked Yasmin.

Jade turned to Sasha and stuck out her hand. "Meet your new yearbook president, Sasha!"

"Congratulations!" exclaimed Cloe.

"Wow, this year, yearbook president. Next year, class president!" said Yasmin.

"Whoa! First things first!" replied Sasha humbly.

As the girls made their way to the school parking lot, Yasmin and Cloe could definitely feel that there was something in the air. Tonight was the night they had all been waiting for, but you wouldn't know it from the way Jade was acting.

"So, you ready to strut your stuff tonight, Jade?" asked Yasmin.

"Yeah . . . I guess," responded Jade.

"I guess?" asked Sasha. "What does that mean?"

"I'm sorry, guys. I just wanted to be yearbook prez so much!" said Jade. "I don't mean to come across like a sore loser, but I know I could've done a bang-up job!"

Sasha looked on, but didn't say a word.

"Hey, I know how you feel," said Cloe. "I didn't win the *Picture Perfect!* contest, either."

"For reals?" asked Sasha.

"Yeah. But don't worry about it! Our time will come," said Cloe to Jade.

"I just hope I'm around when it does," joked Jade. "And one more thing . . ."

The girls looked on with concern. "Shotgun!" exclaimed Jade as she jumped into the front seat of Cloe's cruiser before Yasmin or Sasha had a chance.

"Okay, gals. Let's get this party started already!" shouted Yasmin as she climbed into the backseat, reached forward, and flipped on the FM radio. "Hit it, Cloe!"

Cloe put the car into drive and cruised out of the parking lot. It was time to look to the night ahead.

chapter two

Less than an hour later, the girls were lounging in the huge marble Jacuzzi at their favorite makeover spot, the Stylin' Salon 'N' Spa.

"Now this *is* heaven," said Cloe over the droning beats of the funkadelic downtempo music playing overhead.

Yasmin pressed a button and the steaming water began to bubble and whirl. "I told you this is what we needed," she said.

"This is what we *always* need," said Sasha.

"Don't get too comfy, Bunny Boo," reminded Cloe. "The night is very young."

"Yeah," added Jade. "And it's gonna be an all-nighter for sure!"

"Tonight's slumber party is gonna be so cool," Cloe said.

"Wait till you see what I have planned," said Yasmin with a twinkle in her eye.

"Do tell!" demanded Cloe.

"Not a chance," replied Yasmin. "You're just going to have to wait."

"I'm sure it's going to be so stylin'," said Sasha.

"You'll see," said Yasmin as she slowly made her way out of the Jacuzzi and began to dry herself off.

"What time is it, anyway?" asked Jade.

Yasmin grabbed her watch. "It's nearly six."

"Nearly six?" shouted Cloe as she reached for her clothes from a nearby locker and began to put them on. "We've got to get a move on. We only have like three hours!"

Sasha and Jade quickly dried themselves off and began to dress.

Minutes later, the girls were walking in the parking lot when they heard a familiar voice echoing in the distance. "Really, ladies, you don't have to make yourselves up for me," shouted the voice. The girls knew immediately who it was.

"You wish!" shouted Jade as she turned to find Dylan approaching, with Cameron close behind.

"Hey, girls," said Cameron. "You gals gettin' ready for the big night tonight?"

"Yeah, we were just gettin' in the zone," said Sasha.

"In the zone?" asked Dylan. "Well, perhaps I can help."

"Ummm . . . perhaps . . . not!" replied Jade with a grin.

"Hey, we heard about what happened," said Cameron. "You definitely deserved to win, Cloe."

"Thanks, Cam," Cloe said.

"Yeah, you too, Jade," said Dylan. An awkward silence came over the group.

"Oh . . . um . . . congrats, Sasha," interrupted Dylan.

"Yeah, congratulations," Cameron said.

"Thanks," said Sasha.

"So . . . what are you guys up to?" asked Yasmin. "You're still going to the dance tonight, right?"

"Of course," replied Cameron. "We were just

checking out some new audio equipment across the street."

"They've got this stylin' new portable CD system!" said Dylan. "You've just gotta check it out!"

"Maybe some other time," said Cloe, looking at her watch. "We've gotta jet!"

"Yeah, we've got a lot to do tonight," said Yasmin.

"Okay, well we'll see you later tonight then," said Cameron.

"Tonight it is," said Sasha. The girls made their way to Cloe's vintage cruiser and jumped in.

"Don't forget to save me a dance, ladies," Dylan yelled back.

Jade smiled and blew Dylan a kiss as Cloe put the car into drive and took off. It was time for a quickie car wash before the big night was officially underway.

After a speedy jaunt across town, Cloe pulled into the Rub-a-Dub Hub, the do-it-yourself car wash.

"Okay, let's make this quick," said Cloe as she jumped out of her car and paid the nearby attendant.

Sasha stepped out of the car and turned her attention to the mud that was caked all over the sides. "I didn't notice it, but you're right, Angel. This car really does need a good wash before tonight. How embarrassing!"

"I've got the inside," said Yasmin. Reaching for a nearby portable vacuum machine, Yasmin began to clean the inside of the cruiser.

"Well, I'm drying this time," said Jade as she grabbed a towel.

Cloe grabbed a sponge. "Okay, Sasha, let's hit it," she said. Sasha grabbed a hose and began to spray down the cruiser.

"Watch where you point that thing," yelled Yasmin as Sasha accidentally almost wet her.

"What?" said Jade. "You're not afraid of a little water, are you?"

Yasmin reached over suddenly and grabbed the hose from Sasha. "Are you?" she said as she playfully sprayed Jade with a stream of water.

"Hey!" yelled Jade.

"Sorry, it must've slipped," Yasmin said with a smile.

Jade quickly grabbed the soapy sponge from Cloe

and tossed it at Yasmin. It smacked her right on the cheek and spattered soap all over her. Jade and the other girls burst out laughing.

"Come on, you guys, we're on a very tight schedule!" said Cloe.

Sasha looked at Yasmin and Jade and smiled. "You know, Angel, you really need to loosen up a bit," Sasha said as she grabbed the hose back from Yasmin and sprayed Cloe with it. Cloe screamed and within seconds, all of the girls were in the middle of an all-out car wash war. Suds flew through the air.

The car wash attendant wasn't amused. He rushed over to the girls. "If you girls don't stop, I'm going to have to ask you to leave," he said angrily.

The girls stopped and looked at one another. They were completely drenched and covered in soap. Suddenly, they burst out laughing.

"Sorry," said Yasmin.

"It's just we forgot to shower today," joked Cloe under her breath.

The girls quickly turned their attention back to the

car and finished it off in no time. When they were done, they jumped into Cloe's now shiny-cool cruiser and sped away.

"That was fun," said Cloe. "I think I needed it."

"Yeah, me too," said Jade.

"We *all* needed it," said Sasha.

"How about we stop for a drive-thru smoothie at Blend It Up! before we head home?" Yasmin suggested.

"We still have a lot of time to get ready for the dance, Cloe," Sasha agreed.

"Yeah, I feel the need for a yummy Peachy Keen Mix-Up!" said Yasmin.

"Okay," said Cloe. "But you're buying!"

"You got it," said Yasmin.

"Cool," said Jade. "Let's hit it."

Cloe made a U-turn and headed back to the smoothie shop. The dance could wait just a little bit longer.

chapter three

Hours later, Cloe was applying some glittery hair gel to her golden blonde hair when her fuzzy phone suddenly rang and lit up. Cloe picked it up and checked the caller ID. It was Jade.

"Hey, girl, what's up?" asked Cloe.

"Bad news . . . I can't go," responded Jade.

Cloe, in a complete state of shock, was speechless.

"Just kidding, Angel!" said Jade as she burst into laughter.

"Not funny!" whined Cloe. "I thought you were serious!"

"Are you crazy? Tonight's the Homecoming dance! Nothing could stop me from going!" responded Jade. "I just called because I wanted to thank you for your support earlier."

"Anytime, Kool Kat!" responded Cloe.

"I also have a little favor to ask . . ." began Jade.

Cloe knew by the tone of Jade's voice that her little favor was most likely a big favor. "Alright, break it down," she said.

"Well, I'm standing in front of my mirror and I'm wearing that burgundy skirt with the stylin' tan halter," said Jade.

"Yeah, I know the one! You're gonna look awesome!" said Cloe.

"Thanks, but something is definitely missing," said Jade.

"Like what?" asked Cloe suspiciously.

"Like that totally-hot glittering gold belt we saw in the mall last week!" responded Jade.

"Oh, right!" responded Cloe, knowing exactly what it was that Jade was about to ask. "So, let me guess—you want to pick it up on the way to the dance?"

"I thought you would never ask!" Jade said, squealing with excitement.

"Alright, let me check with the girls. Hold on," said Cloe as she clicked the flash button on her phone and conference-called Yasmin.

"Hello?" whispered the voice on the other end of the phone.

"Hi! It's me and Jade. Did we wake you?" asked Cloe.

"Don't be ridiculous! I'm baking a seven-layer cake for tonight and I don't want to make any loud noises," responded Yasmin.

"Umm . . . I don't get it," responded Cloe.

"It's in the oven, silly," said Yasmin. "If I make any loud noises, my seven-layer could fall and become a two-layer!"

"Oh! Of course!" laughed Cloe.

"So, what's up?" asked Yasmin.

"Jade wants to make a quick stop at the mall before the dance. Can you get ready sooner?" asked Cloe.

"As long as we can stop at Kiss 'N' Make-up. I've got to pick up some lip gloss pronto!" said Yasmin.

"Fine by me," Jade chimed in.

"Okay, hold on. Let me get Sasha on the phone," said Cloe as she hit the flash button again and speed-dialed Sasha.

"Hey, Cloe! What's up?" said the voice on the other line.

"It's not just me, Bunny," responded Cloe.

"Hey, girl!" interrupted Yasmin.

"Hello, Ms. Yearbook President," said Jade.

"Hey, ladies. What's going on?" asked Sasha.

"Do you mind if we make a quick stop at the mall before the big dance tonight? Yasmin and Jade need to stop for some last-minutes," asked Cloe.

"No worries!" responded Sasha. "I'm in desperate need of a pair of earrings to top off my outfit."

"Great," responded Cloe. "We'll pick you up in forty-five minutes!"

"Forty-five minutes? I gotta go!" gasped Sasha as she quickly hung up.

"I'll pick you gals up in half an hour," said Cloe to Jade and Yasmin.

"Okay," said Yasmin.

"Oh, but Yas, before you go, just one more thing," said Jade.

"Yeah?" replied Yasmin.

"Extra icing!" blurted Jade.

Cloe and Yasmin both laughed at the same time. This was definitely going to be a night to remember.

■ ■ ■ ■

Later that evening, the girls found themselves at the mall in the middle of a last-minute shopping spree.

"I think these are for me!" said Sasha in excitement as she held up a pair of glittering gemstone-studded earrings.

"Wow! That would definitely top off your look," responded Yasmin.

Sasha was wearing an incredible black jean mini with a golden-orange striped top that made her brown eyes shimmer and shine.

"Cool! Buy it and then let's hit the make-up shop for Yasmin," said Cloe. The girls just smiled. It was obvious that even though Cloe didn't win the *Picture Perfect!*

contest, she was totally psyched about going to the dance.

Minutes later, the girls were rushing in and out of a sea of shoppers on their way to their favorite make-up store, Kiss 'N' Make-up. As they moved, they passed all the stores they normally loved to frequent.

"Oh, look, they've got new puppies at the pet store!" shouted Jade. "Let's stop!"

"We can't, Jade!" said Sasha. "Don't wanna be late to the dance."

Jade knew what Sasha was saying was right. But deep down, she couldn't help but feel a little resentment at being bossed around by the new yearbook president. And even though she was trying to be cool, Mr. Kelly's words still echoed in her head. As she passed the pet store, she quickly waved hello.

The girls arrived at the make-up shop and Yasmin rushed in.

"Five minutes!" yelled Cloe as the other girls followed her in.

Yasmin ran to the back of the store and pointed to the red, shimmering lip gloss she needed so badly. "Yes,

Hearts Afire!" she said to the woman behind the counter.

"What? Hot date?" joked the woman.

"Something like that," Yasmin said, smiling.

Across the store, Jade and Cloe were trying on the latest colors in blush when Sasha suddenly called out, "We've got to book! It's nearly eight!"

Yasmin quickly paid the woman and then the girls feverishly sprinted in the direction of their favorite clothing store, Chix.

"Please make it quick, Jade," said Cloe, slightly out of breath.

"No problem," responded Jade. "I saw it just a couple of days ago. I know exactly where it is!"

Cloe, Sasha, Yasmin, and Jade ran down the escalator and into Chix. Jade ran to the accessories section to pick up her belt, while the other girls suddenly stopped short at the up-front display. *New fashions*, they thought as it became more than clear that the latest fall fashions had just arrived and were being set up by a store clerk.

"Check out this funky frilly blouse!" squealed Yasmin.

"You would so look like a poet in that, Yas!" replied Cloe as she grabbed a pair of cooler-than-ice distressed jeans. "Funkalish!"

Sasha, who had been keeping an eye on the time, forgot everything when she saw a pale green skirt with a matching halter on a nearby mannequin. "Look at that!" she said. "Totally stylin'!"

The girls reached and grabbed at more and more clothes. Jade slowly made her way back to the group. "They don't have my belt. What am I going to . . ." she began as she suddenly caught a glimpse of the coolest-looking fire-engine red jacket she had ever seen. "Funkadelic!" she exclaimed, reaching for it to try it on.

Overhead, a melodic chime sounded throughout the mall. "The mall will be closing in twenty minutes. Please make your final selection and purchase your items right away," said a voice over the chime. But the girls didn't hear a thing. They were too busy trying on clothes!

As the announcement was repeated, Sasha jetted into the dressing room with a stack of cool items. Cloe followed her seconds later with even more stylin' fashions.

Yasmin and Jade followed them both with tons more.

Minutes later, the girls were trying on the coolest fashion looks.

"You girls ready?" asked Cloe, opening the dressing room curtain dramatically and stepping out. She was wearing an almost floor-length cotton dress that looked like it would've been perfect for a summer night out and about, but the totally cool autumn-red colors and fashionable angular cut gave it an end-of-the-year, dress-up and dance flair.

"Lookin' good!" responded Yasmin. "But check this out!" Yasmin stepped out in the hottest European-styled vintage number that included a Victorian blouse and woven-gray satin skirt. It made her look as if she was a top model from the not-too-distant past.

"Not too shabby, but are you ready for the next big thing?" asked Sasha suggestively.

"Bring it on!" said Jade.

Slowly, Sasha sashayed out in the pale green skirt and halter she had seen displayed on the mannequin only moments before.

"Wow, nice!" responded Cloe.

"I think I may even wear this to the dance tonight!" said Sasha.

"What about you, Kool Kat?" asked Yasmin.

"I'm not sure which outfit to wear. They all look too good!" replied Jade.

"Well, if you're going to take your time, I'm goin' back in for another outfit!" said Cloe as she darted back into the dressing room to try on something else.

"I think I'll second that motion," said Sasha as she did the same.

As Cloe, Sasha, Jade, and Yasmin changed outfits and chattered away, an announcement came over the intercom system once again. "The mall will be closing in five minutes. Please make your final selection and purchase your items right away," said the voice over a melodic chime. But once again, the girls didn't hear a thing.

"Okay, I think I'm ready!" said Jade, her voice squeaking in delight.

"Strut your stuff, girl!" said Yasmin.

As all three girls opened their curtains to catch a glimpse, Jade jumped out of her dressing room and began to dance down the aisle like an early '80s new waver. Dressed in black jeans, a striped black-and-white halter, and the red jacket she saw earlier, she was the ultimate retro-chic chick.

"Jade, how do you always manage to look so good?" Cloe asked.

"It's a gift," replied Jade, twirling in front of the mirror, beaming in delight.

"You've got to wear that tonight!" said Yasmin.

"I'm never taking it off!" said Jade, when from out of nowhere, she gasped.

"What is it?" asked an alarmed Sasha.

"I still need a belt to wear with this outfit!" Jade said.

"Ooooohhhhh . . . here we go again . . ." began Yasmin, when suddenly . . . everything went dark!

"Ahhhhhh!" screamed Sasha.

"Hey, who turned out the lights?" asked Yasmin. "Is it a blackout?"

Jade kept her cool and grabbed her nearby key-chain flashlight. She pressed a button and a small light illuminated the darkness around her. Quickly, she made her way through the blackness, out of the dressing room area and into the main store. Even with only minimal lighting, she knew Chix like the back of her hand.

"This is crazy! How do they expect us to buy if we can't see what we're buying?" asked Yasmin.

Sasha could feel her heart beating in her chest. She looked down at her watch and pressed the light to see what time it was. "Guys!" she shrieked. "It's nine-thirty!"

"That's impossible!" responded Yasmin. "We just got here like twenty minutes ago!"

"Are you saying we're missing the dance?" asked Cloe.

"No . . . I'm not . . ." replied Sasha. "I'm saying . . ."

"The mall's closed!" interrupted Jade suddenly.

"What?" gasped Yasmin. "That's impossible!"

"And we're locked in!" continued Jade.

chapter four

Suddenly, the girls were filled with panic.

"Locked in?" exclaimed Cloe.

Sasha quickly rushed into the darkness. "We've got to get out of here!" she said, but was instantly stopped by a door in the dressing room. "Where am I?"

Jade raced over to Sasha and grabbed her hand. "I'm right here, Bunny. Don't freak."

"We're gonna miss the dance!" said Cloe, realizing the horror of the situation.

"We *are* missing the dance," Yasmin corrected her.

"Look, everybody grab an arm and let's move to the front of the store. I'm sure we can catch a security guard if we move fast," said Jade.

The girls grabbed hands and slowly moved through the blackness, making sure not to knock into a nearby mannequin or bump into a wall. After a few moments, the girls reached the glass doors at the front of the store.

"Where are all the lights?" asked Jade as she looked out through the glass doors and into the mall.

"What should we do?" asked Cloe.

"Why don't we try yelling?" suggested Sasha.

"Okay," responded Yasmin. "Let's do it."

All at once, the girls began yelling. And screaming. And even banging. Over and over again. But nobody answered.

"Get us out of here!" Sasha shouted, but still there was no response.

"Oh my gosh! We really are trapped," said Cloe.

Jade had an idea. She let go of the girls and walked away into the darkness. "Hey, Yas," she began, "do you remember that time last month when we were the first ones here and they hadn't opened the store yet?"

"Ummm . . . yeah. We were waiting just outside here," said Yasmin, gesturing beyond the glass doors.

"Right," said Jade. "Remember what the salesgirl did before she let us in?"

"I think so," responded Yasmin. "Didn't she pull a

lever or something over by the sleepwear section?"

"Exactly!" said Jade. "Look what I found!" Jade shined her key-chain flashlight onto an inconspicuous lever and pulled it down. The front glass doors miraculously opened up.

"You did it!" shouted Sasha.

"Okay, now let's get out of here!" said Cloe. "We gotta make that dance!"

"I'll lead the way," shouted Jade, flashlight in hand. The girls quickly raced to the front of the mall. As they did, they couldn't help but notice how quiet everything had become. It seemed like only moments ago that the mall had been alive with music and lights. And shoppers galore. Now it was like a deserted ghost town.

"Okay, we should turn left here," said Jade, indicating which direction led to the mall entrance.

"No, not that way," disagreed Sasha. "It's this way."

"I know where I'm going," said Jade defensively.

"No, you don't," replied Sasha.

"Yes, I do, Ms. President!" snapped Jade. She

hadn't even realized she was going to say that!

"What's that supposed to mean?" asked Sasha.

"You always have to be the leader!" said Jade.

"Well, if it wasn't for you, we wouldn't be in this mess!" yelled Sasha.

"Me?" replied Jade.

"Yeah! You're the one who wanted to come to the mall before the dance for your stupid belt!" shouted Sasha.

"And what about your earrings?" Jade asked.

"Ladies! Stop it!" interrupted Yasmin. "You're both overreacting. If we just keep going straight, we should be there in no time."

Sasha and Jade looked at each other.

"Look, we need to stick together. Let's not fall apart now, okay? If you guys have stuff to talk about, let's deal with it *after* we find our way out of here," said Cloe decisively.

"You're right," said Jade after a moment. "I'm sorry, Sasha."

"It's cool," replied Sasha. "I'm sorry, too."

The girls continued to walk. After a few minutes, they

came upon the big steel, glass doors of the mall entrance. Sasha reached out to open them, but they didn't budge.

"Try it again," said Yasmin.

Sasha, this time joined by Cloe and Jade, pushed and pulled harder on the doors. "It's no use," responded Sasha. "They won't budge. We're locked in."

Yasmin reached into her pocket and pulled out her cell phone. "We need to call somebody now!"

"Call Cameron and the guys," said Jade. "They'll get somebody to get us out."

"They're at the dance," said Sasha.

"*Everybody's* at the dance," said Cloe.

"It doesn't matter," interrupted Yasmin. "There's no signal."

"What are we going to do now?" asked Cloe.

The situation was going from bad to worse. And even though the girls had one another, they found themselves feeling very alone.

"Looks like we're going to have to wait for somebody to let us out," Sasha announced.

"How? Nobody even knows we're here!" said Cloe.

"I know. We're going to have to wait until the morning, when they reopen," responded Sasha.

"Do you mean . . . ?" began Yasmin.

"We're going to have to spend the night," Sasha said.

"But our slumber party!" said Yasmin.

"What about Homecoming?" asked Cloe.

Sasha's silence said it all. The girls now realized the gravity of the situation. Slowly, they turned to find the empty, darkened mall behind them. A sound echoed in the blackness.

"What was that?" asked Cloe.

"Oh, I hope this mall isn't haunted," said Yasmin.

"Stop your stories, girl," said Sasha.

"We've got to find the lights!" said Jade as she looked down at the key-chain flashlight she was holding. "The batteries are running out."

"Well, you found the door lever at Chix," said Cloe. "Any idea where the lights are?"

"Not exactly," responded Jade. "But maybe we should start walking. They've got to be around somewhere."

The girls grabbed hands and began to walk back into the mall, into the darkness.

"I never thought I would say this," began Sasha, "but I can't wait to get out of this mall."

"Yeah, but this *is* gonna make a great story once we're out," said Yasmin.

"*If* we get out," said Cloe.

"I think this could be fun," said Jade.

The girls stopped and looked at Jade.

"What?" asked Sasha.

"Think about it: a night in the mall!" replied Jade. "It's like a dream come true!"

"She must be in a state of shock," whispered Cloe to Yasmin.

"This is gonna be fun, you'll see," said Jade.

"Oh, now I remember!" said Cloe. "Jade, let me borrow your flashlight." Jade handed Cloe her flashlight, and Cloe raced off into the darkness.

"Where are you going?" yelled Sasha.

"Cloe! Cloe!" yelled Yasmin.

"Give me one minute!" responded Cloe. A moment

later, a low hum echoed in the darkness. "I think I did it." Suddenly, from every corner of every store, the mall became filled with light. In the middle of the mall, a huge golden carousel filled with golden ornamental horses and carriages began to spin in time to music. The girls turned to find Cloe in a booth several feet away, wearing a huge smile.

"You did it!" squealed Yasmin.

"I guess it was my turn to save the day," Cloe joked. "I remembered that when I was younger, I got lost in the mall. The security guard brought me here, to the control booth."

"Cool!" said Sasha.

"Hey, guys, come on!" said Jade as she ran ahead and jumped onto the spinning carousel. "Think about it: a night in the mall!"

"I guess there could be worse places to be stuck," said Yasmin as she took a running leap and joined Jade on the merry-go-round. Both Yasmin and Jade began to laugh.

"There's got to be a way out of here," said Sasha.

"But, for right now, I think I could go for some fun!" Sasha ran to the carousel and joined the girls.

"Come on, Cloe!" yelled Jade.

"But the dance . . ." whined Cloe.

"Forget the dance!" said Jade. "This is gonna be way more superstylin' than the dance!"

"Jade's right. We can do whatever we want!" said Yasmin.

"Clooooooeeeee . . ." sang Sasha. "You can *try on* whatever you want!"

Cloe thought a moment and slowly a smile appeared on her face. An all-night fashion show. Nobody to rush her. This *was* a once-in-a-lifetime opportunity. Besides, what choice did she have? "Okay, I'm in!" Cloe exclaimed. The party of the year was just beginning.

chapter five

About an hour later, the girls were knee-deep in the coolest cosmetics at Kiss 'N' Make-up. So they were stuck in the mall for a night: It didn't mean they couldn't make the best out of a difficult situation.

"How does this look?" asked Cloe, pointing to her ruby red cheeks and the Violet Flare blush that colored them.

"Pretty good to me," said Yasmin. "Too bad we can't actually buy anything."

"Why not?" asked Cloe.

"Who would we pay?" responded Sasha.

"Oh . . . I guess you're right!" said Cloe. "We'll just have to think of tonight as the ultimate window-shopping experience."

"Yeah, and we're stuck in the window," joked Sasha.

Yasmin opened a sampler bottle of perfume and splashed it on her neck. "You know, I'm a little hungry."

Cloe gasped. "What are we gonna do for food?"

"It's called the food court," responded Jade. "But we can't eat at a time like this! We haven't even hit the department stores yet."

"I'm a little hungry myself," said Cloe as she applied a dash of eyeliner to her beautiful blue eyes. "Let's head on over and see what's on the menu."

"Sounds like a plan," said Sasha. "But I think I'm gonna freshen up first at the salon before I head on over."

"The salon sounds perfect," said Jade. "Count me in!"

"Okay, we can meet you two there," said Yasmin, wiping the make-up off her face.

"Okay. Say in half an hour?" said Sasha.

"Cool," said Cloe.

Cloe and Yasmin quickly cleaned up and started out into the empty mall.

"See you there," yelled Yasmin. "And don't be late!"

Jade and Sasha quickly cleaned up and headed out

into the mall soon after. Within minutes, they had made their way to the local hair salon, the Stylin' Hair Studio. As they entered the store, Sasha switched on the overhead lights and Jade turned on the music.

"You wanna go first?" asked Jade.

"Okay. But just a simple wash and condition is fine," responded Sasha. "We don't want to keep Cloe and Yas waiting too long."

Sasha sat down in a nearby salon chair and rested her head against the sink. Her beautiful brown hair fell gently into the sink.

"Okay, I'm ready," she said.

"Would you like your hair to smell like apples or kiwis?" asked Jade, holding up two different bottles of conditioner.

"You decide," said Sasha.

"Kiwis it is," said Jade as she flipped on the sink and began dousing Sasha's hair with warm water.

■ ■ ■ ■

Meanwhile, Cloe and Yasmin were making their way

to the food court. They had never seen the mall so empty. It was kinda cool, they thought, not having to shove their way through long lines and turtle walkers to get to where they wanted to go. But it was just so weird. As they were ascending the escalator, Cloe spotted the huge store window of Fashion Friendz-y!, the funky fashion store that was second only to Chix.

"I just don't get it. This store is like practically the coolest store in the mall, yet this window display is so snooze-ville," said Cloe, referring to the out-of-fashion summer colors and disarrayed arrangement on display.

"Well, maybe they need the Cloe touch," said Yasmin.

Cloe thought for a moment about what she would do to make the display a winner. Since autumn was just beginning, she imagined gorgeous brown and red streamers hanging from the ceiling in the shapes of leaves, with a cozy park bench nestled in the middle of the window, surrounded by mannequins walking to and fro, as if it were a lazy afternoon in October. But just as quickly as Cloe's decorative display came to mind, so did the memory of losing the *Picture Perfect!* contest at school. Despite being stuck in the mall for a night and missing out on the big dance, for Cloe, losing the *Picture Perfect!* contest still haunted her.

"Yeah, like I could help," responded Cloe.

"Don't be so hard on yourself, Cloe," said Yasmin. "You know you could make this window rock!"

"Thanks, Princess," Cloe said. She and Yasmin continued to walk. "Can we talk about something else?"

"Like how we're trapped in here for the night?" Yasmin joked.

"Much better!" responded Cloe with a laugh.

Yasmin suddenly stopped in her tracks. "Angel!" she said. "Look!"

There, standing not ten feet from them, was a row of pay phones hanging on a wall. "Come on!" Cloe yelled.

"Why didn't we think of this sooner?" asked Yasmin.

The girls ran over to the pay phones. Yasmin picked up the receiver of one of the phones, and Cloe handed her some change. Yasmin smiled and put the receiver to her ear.

"Oh, no!" Yasmin said. "There's no dial tone."

Cloe grabbed another phone and placed it to her ear. "No dial tone here, either!"

Both girls looked at each other and sighed.

"These phones never work," said Yasmin.

"They were supposed to fix them weeks ago," said Cloe, dejected. "But that would've been too easy."

■ ■ ■ ■

Back at the Stylin' Hair Studio, Sasha was finishing up Jade's hair wash.

"Do we really have to go?" joked Jade as she wrapped a towel around her head and sat up from the washbasin. The relaxed look on her face said it all.

"Aren't you hungry yet?" asked Sasha.

"Yes, but with all that fruity conditioning in my hair, I feel like I've already had dinner!" Jade responded.

"Crazy, girl!" said Sasha. "Come on, Cloe and Yas are waiting. Let's clean up and hit it or we're gonna be late!"

"Okay, let me just dry my hair," said Jade as she

grabbed a nearby hair-dryer and began to work it.

After several minutes, Jade's hair was dry and the Stylin' Hair Studio was shiny clean. As the girls were leaving, Jade turned to Sasha and flashed a curious smile.

"What are you grinning at?" asked Sasha.

"Race ya?" said Jade.

"You're on!" replied Sasha.

"On your mark, get set, go!" yelled Jade as both girls bolted at full speed in the direction of the food court. But after only a couple of seconds, Jade suddenly stopped short.

"What? You're giving up already?" said Sasha.

"You wish," joked Jade as she pointed to the floor overhead. "Look!"

Sasha looked up and saw that just above where she was standing was the pet store from earlier.

"Let's make a quickie stop," said Jade.

"But we're running late," said Sasha.

"Come on! Where's your sense of adventure?" asked Jade.

Sasha thought a moment and then smiled. "Okay, but let's be quick."

Sasha and Jade made their way to a nearby elevator and got in. Jade pressed Level Two, and the doors closed. The elevator began its quick ascent up, when all of a sudden, it jerked. And then stopped. The girls grabbed each other and gave a scream.

"What just happened?" asked Sasha.

Jade reached over and pressed several different elevator buttons, but the elevator didn't move. "I think we're stuck," whispered Jade.

"What's that?" asked Sasha, pointing to an orange blinking light underneath the floor display.

"It says 'Malfunction,' " said Jade.

"Malfunction? What are we gonna do?" asked Sasha.

Jade opened up the emergency control panel. "Don't panic."

"Too late!" squealed Sasha as she raced to the elevator doors and began to bang. After a moment, she stopped and turned to Jade. "Is it me, or is it getting hot in here?"

"I think it's you," said Jade. "Look, it says that all

somebody has to do is flick a switch for the malfunction to be fixed."

"Well, that's great!" replied Sasha. "Flick it and let's get out of here!"

"I would, but the switch can be found only in one place," said Jade.

"Where?" asked Sasha.

"On the outside of the elevator," sighed Jade.

"You mean . . . ?" asked Sasha.

"We're stuck in here until somebody finds us!" said Jade.

Sasha's eyes widened. She leaned up against the elevator wall and then slowly let herself slide down. "Here we go again," she said under her breath.

■ ■ ■ ■

On the other side of the mall, Cloe and Yasmin were already walking to the food court when, from almost out of nowhere, a low rumbling sound could be heard coming from the direction of Cloe.

"I guess somebody's hungry," announced Yasmin.

"Excuse me," said Cloe as she grabbed her stomach and blushed.

"Wow! I never noticed just how many choices there are here!" said Yasmin. "I think I'm in the mood for pizza. With the works!"

"Sounds delish!" responded Cloe. "But I think I'm in the mood for a good ol' fashioned burger, fries, and an ice-cold vanilla milkshake!"

"Mmmmmm . . . that's sounds good, too!" said Yasmin.

"Or maybe I'm in the mood for some Chinese-style," said Cloe. "Orange chicken sounds yummy!"

"Maybe a fresh salad would hit the spot!" said Yasmin, now walking faster.

"I say we make it all!" said Cloe. "That way, we can pick and choose!"

"Good idea!" yelled Yasmin.

The girls stopped by every restaurant choice and perused each of the many fine delicacies the food court had to offer. From the burger joint and pizza parlor to the salad station and ice-cream stand, the girls just couldn't wait to start cookin'.

"Hey, where're Jade and Sasha?" asked Cloe.

"Yeah, where are they? They should be here by now," said Yasmin.

"Bunny? Kool Kat?" Cloe called out. But there was no response. "Maybe they're still freshening up."

"Maybe," said Yasmin. "But still, when was the last time Sasha was late for anything?"

"Do you think they found a way out?" asked Cloe.

"No. They would've come looking for us," said Yasmin. A pause came over the girls. "Right?"

"Of course they would've," Cloe assured her. "They're probably on their way as we speak. Let's go look."

Sasha and Jade have to be close by, they thought. There was no reason to worry. They were probably just having a good time. All they had to do was find them.

chapter six

Jade and Sasha sat side by side in the elevator. They were both exhausted from yelling for help. They knew that eventually Cloe or Yasmin would pass by and find them. It was only a question of time.

"How long has it been?" asked Jade.

"About half an hour," responded Sasha.

"I hope they find us," said Jade.

"Of course they'll find us," said Sasha sharply as she stood up to get a better view of the mall.

"I am so hungry," said Jade.

"Yeah, so am I," responded Sasha.

"I can't believe we're stuck in here," said Jade.

"Look, don't blame yourself," said Sasha. "You didn't know."

"Blame myself?" said Jade, standing up. "What do you mean, 'blame myself'?"

"You know what I mean," responded Sasha. "If we had just done what I had said, and stuck to the plan, we wouldn't be in this mess."

Jade turned beet red with anger. "You're not serious, are you?" she said. "It wasn't my fault the elevator got stuck! I just pressed the button. That's all."

"Yeah, but you're the one who just had to visit the pet store," Sasha said abruptly.

"You know, I am so sick and tired of you thinking you know what's best!" Jade shot back. "It's always 'you do this' and 'you do that'! Who made you the boss, anyway?"

"Mr. Kelly did, remember?" Sasha snapped back.

Jade was speechless. Sasha knew she had crossed the line, but when she reached out to grab Jade's hand, Jade pulled it away.

"I didn't mean that," said Sasha. "Please forgive me, Jade."

"Yes, you did," whispered Jade, clearly shaken. "Don't talk to me!"

Sasha slid down on the ground next to Jade.

"You're right, Jade," she said. "You didn't do anything wrong. The truth is, I'm just very scared. This whole night has really freaked me out. But since the beginning, *you've* been taking it all in stride. I mean, this is *fun* for you."

"Sometimes, you've just got to let go and roll with it," whispered Jade.

"I'm sorry for saying those things to you. They aren't true."

"Bunny, I've been sensitive a little, too," said Jade. "I felt totally dissed when Mr. Kelly elected you over me. And deep down, I kinda resented you for it. For that, *I'm* sorry."

"It's okay, Kool Kat," said Sasha. "I would be honored if you would help me out next year."

"Of course I will," said Jade as she reached over and hugged Sasha. Just as she did, Jade caught a glimpse of Cloe and Yasmin walking in the distance. "Look!" she yelled.

"It's them!" said Sasha.

"Hey!" yelled Jade. "We're over here!"

But Cloe and Yasmin didn't react.

"Cloe! Yasmin!" yelled Sasha. "Get us out of here!"

"They can't hear us," said Jade when there was still no reaction.

Both Jade and Sasha began to jump up and down and flail their arms wildly as Cloe and Yasmin walked nearer to the elevator.

"We're not getting their attention!" yelled Sasha in a panic. "They're going to pass us."

"Bang on the windows," said Jade.

The girls banged on the windows just as Yasmin and Cloe were about to pass. But after a few moments, both girls passed by the elevator, unaware that Jade and Sasha were trapped inside.

"How could they not hear or see us?" said Sasha as she turned to Jade, defeated.

"These walls must be soundproofed," responded Jade. "Looks like we're gonna be in here a while longer."

"I know, I know: Roll with the punches," said Sasha.

"Exactly," said Jade as both girls sat down and prepared themselves for an even longer wait. But then, above the doorway, the floor light indicator lit up.

"What the . . . ?" said Jade, confused, as she jumped up and caught sight of Cloe, not one foot in front of her, pressing the button for the elevator.

"She's trying to use the elevator!" squealed Jade.

"She still doesn't know we're in here!" said Sasha.

Both girls began to jump up and down in an attempt to get her attention.

"Cloe, we're in here!" said Sasha and Jade, when suddenly Yasmin jumped into view, pointing. Cloe looked up and saw the girls behind the glass doors.

"There you are!" yelled Cloe as she pressed the elevator's buttons in an attempt to open them.

"It's broken!" yelled Jade.

"We have to tell them what to do!" Sasha said to Jade.

Jade turned to Cloe and Yasmin and yelled, "Press the red button!" But the girls couldn't hear what she was saying.

"Press the red button!" yelled Sasha, but still Cloe and Yasmin couldn't make out what she was saying.

But then Jade had an idea. She reached into her

pocket and pulled out a tube of lipstick and began writing a message on the glass window.

"What does it say?" asked Cloe, trying to read the message that was being spelled out backwards, like a mirror image.

"Push . . . the . . . red . . . button," read Yasmin slowly.

"They must mean this one," said Cloe, pointing to the emergency button on the outside door. Cloe pressed the button and the elevator jerked. And then the doors magically opened.

"I can breathe again!" shouted Sasha as she jumped out of the elevator and hugged Cloe.

"Are you okay?" asked Yasmin.

"Barely!" exclaimed Jade.

"We thought you guys had left," said Cloe.

"And leave you here? Alone? No way!" said Sasha, stepping out of the elevator. "We were just doing what we do best!"

"Which is?" asked Yasmin.

"Getting trapped!" responded Jade. The girls

laughed. "Now, how about that dinner!"

"Good idea," said Cloe.

The girls quickly made their way back to the food court.

■ ■ ■ ■

"Wow, where do we begin?" said Yasmin, looking at all the food choices before her.

"I think I want pizza," said Jade.

"Me, too," said Cloe.

"Well, I think I want a burger!" said Yasmin.

"A burger sounds perfect," said Sasha.

"Then let's get to it," said Jade.

The girls slapped hands in excitement and each girl hit the kitchen of her choice.

Jade and Cloe stopped at their favorite place for quick Italian food, Piece o' Pizza, the hands-down, best pizza joint in town. As soon as they got there, Jade fired up the brick oven and Cloe broke out the mozzarella cheese, tomato sauce, and veggies. Jade grabbed a mound of dough from the refrigerator and began twisting and turning it to thin it out. After a couple of minutes, she began throwing it high into the air.

"Are you sure you know what you're doing?" yelled Cloe.

"Are you kidding?" replied Jade. "I've seen them do this a thousand times." But just as Jade said this, she threw the dough so high into the air that it smacked into the ceiling and got stuck there. Cloe, who was cutting up veggies, heard the noise and turned to see Jade staring up at the ceiling.

"Oops!" said Jade, reaching into the refrigerator for another mound of dough. "Let me try that again."

Meanwhile, across the court, Sasha was grilling up burgers and cooking fries at the coolest fifties diner in town, the Krazy-Kool Retro-Café. With cool rockabilly tunes playing overhead, Yasmin was trying her hand at the shake machine.

"Hey, Bunny, what flavor you cravin'?" yelled Yasmin from the ice-cream fountain in front.

"Strawberry!" replied Sasha.

Yasmin added a cup of milk, a scoop of ice cream,

and a cup of special strawberry flavoring to the blender cup. "This is gonna be the best tastin' shake you've ever had!" yelled Yasmin as she flicked on the blender switch full throttle. But just as she did, the blender shot up and its contents sprayed out without warning all over Yasmin. "Ahhh!" Yasmin screamed, reaching to flick the blender off.

Sasha, hearing the scream, ran to Yasmin and found her covered in pink goo. "That's got to be your *sweetest* look yet!" joked Sasha.

"Not funny," responded Yasmin.

"What happened?" asked Sasha.

"I forgot to put the top on," admitted Yasmin.

Sasha broke into a laughing fit.

"Hey, what's that smell?" asked Yasmin.

"Ohhh! My burgers!" shouted Sasha as she ran back into the kitchen and grabbed a nearby spatula. "Oh, no!" she yelled.

"What is it?" said Yasmin. She ran back in and found Sasha holding up two burnt hamburger patties.

"Too hot to handle, Bunny Boo?" joked Yasmin.

"Not funny," responded Sasha.

■ ■ ■ ■

It took less than twenty minutes for the girls to finish up and meet up in the middle of the food court for the meal they had so been craving. While the pizzas were cooking, Cloe grabbed what she could and set the table in the style of a fancy café, complete with folded napkins, pastel flowers, and candles.

"Very impressive, Angel," said Jade as she carried two pizzas to the table.

"Yes, looks very chic," agreed Sasha as she arrived with a tray of sizzlin' burgers and fries. Yasmin followed behind with a tray of drinks.

"Thanks, guys!" responded Cloe.

"What happened to you?" Jade asked Yasmin.

"I had a little accident with the shake machine," Yasmin said.

"I know what you mean," replied Jade. "Pizza is a

lot harder to make than it looks."

The girls sat down. Jade lifted up her cup of water and proposed a toast. "Well, here's to a night we'll definitely never forget!"

"And here's to making the best out of any situation," added Sasha.

"You got that right," said Yasmin.

"The food looks so good!" said Cloe.

"Let's dig in!" shouted Jade.

The girls began to eat, when suddenly Cloe heard a sound coming from behind her. She turned to see what it was, and was suddenly struck with fear. "Nobody move," she said.

Confused, Yasmin and Jade turned to see what had caught Cloe's eye and instantly froze; because standing there only a few feet away from them were three growling Doberman pinscher dogs.

"Oh, no!" screamed Jade. The dogs, hearing Jade, began to growl more viciously.

Sasha turned her head and caught a glimpse of the

commotion. Seeing the dogs, she immediately jumped up in a panic and was about to make a bolt for it when Jade quickly grabbed her hand.

"Don't move," Jade said.

"What are we gonna do?" whispered Cloe.

"I say we run for it," responded Yasmin.

"No, let's wait," said Sasha.

"Are you crazy, Bunny?" responded Yasmin. "They're gonna jump us if we just wait."

The girls stood there, frozen, fighting the impulse to run. Why there were three growling dogs was a total mystery. But that didn't matter now. All that mattered to the girls was a safe getaway. But was it even possible?

chapter seven

As the girls stood motionless, the dogs began to edge closer to them.

"Where . . . did . . . they come from?" whispered Yasmin.

"They're probably the mall's guard dogs," responded Sasha.

"Guard dogs?" responded Cloe.

"Don't look them in the eye," said Yasmin, staring at the ground in front of her.

"We need to distract them," said Jade. "And then jam out of here."

"I'm scared," whispered Cloe.

Slowly, Sasha picked up a piece of pizza from the table. "Yas, grab a burger. They're probably hungry." Yasmin grabbed a burger and Jade grabbed a slice of pizza.

"Okay, on the count of three," began Sasha, "we're gonna throw this at them."

The dogs suddenly began to bark violently.

"One . . ." began Sasha.

"Two . . ." continued Yasmin.

"Three!" shouted Jade. Without warning, the girls chucked the food at the dogs and caught them off guard. The dogs lunged forward, but quickly pulled back upon smelling the delectable aroma of the food. Turning, they pounced on the burger and pizza slices.

"Now's our chance!" yelled Sasha.

"Run!" shouted Jade.

As fast as they possibly could, the girls took off into the mall. Cloe turned to see if the dogs were chasing her. Instead, they were still in the food court, eating the food that was thrown. "It's working!" she yelled.

"Keep running!" yelled Sasha, making her way down the escalator and onto the first floor. Finally, they made it to the other end of the mall.

"I think we've lost them," said Jade, turning to see if the dogs were near.

The girls sat on a nearby bench and caught their breath.

"Could this night get any worse?" asked Sasha.

"What are we gonna do if they come back?" asked Cloe. "Make them dessert?"

The girls laughed. But just as they did, a loud bark echoed through the mall. The girls jumped up.

"Oh, no! They're coming for us!" said Cloe.

"Stay here," said Sasha as she ran back to see what direction the barks had come from. Sasha reached the top of the escalator and scanned the mall. "I think they left," she shouted back to the girls.

"Are you sure?" yelled Cloe.

"Yeah," responded Sasha, now walking back to the group. "They're nowhere to be found." But just as she said this, the three growling Dobermans appeared behind her on the escalator.

"Bunny! Run!" shouted Cloe.

Sasha turned around and caught sight of the dogs as they were making their way off the escalator. Quickly, she turned and ran toward a nearby toy store. The dogs tumbled off the escalator and instead of rushing after Sasha, they made a dash for Cloe, Jade, and Yasmin, who were already running in the opposite direction.

"They're coming! Where are we gonna go?" shouted Jade, running at top speed.

Just then, Yasmin tripped and fell.

"Princess!" yelled Cloe as she quickly stuck out her hand and lifted Yasmin up. Both girls turned to see that the dogs were closing in.

"They're gaining on us!" yelled Jade.

"Let's duck in here!" yelled Yasmin, pointing to the local movie-plex.

Quickly, the girls ran past the main gates and threw the front doors wide open. They filed in and slammed the doors closed just as one of the dogs lunged at Jade.

"Hold it closed!" yelled Jade over the barking of the dogs.

"What happened to Sasha?" asked Yasmin.

"Don't worry, I saw her duck into the toy store," said Cloe.

"Leave it to Bunny Boo to play games at a time like

this!" joked Jade.

The girls jammed a planter in front of the door and backed away.

"That should hold them out," said Yasmin.

"But we still need to get out of here!" reminded Cloe.

"Yeah, we have to catch up with Sasha," said Jade.

The girls thought for a moment. How could they get out? And, more importantly, how could they get the dogs in? They definitely needed to trap them, but how could they do it without getting hurt? The girls paced the lobby of the movie theater.

"Okay," started Jade. "Let's keep it simple. When I give the signal, I want you to open the door."

"Are you crazy?" responded Cloe. "I'm not letting those dogs in here."

"When they come in," explained Jade, "we'll jump out!"

"And what happens if we get stuck in here with them?" asked Yasmin.

"We won't!" said Jade defiantly.

"How can we make sure they don't attack us?" asked Cloe.

Jade thought a moment and then approached the candy counter. She grabbed three huge tubs of leftover popcorn and handed them to the girls. "We can distract them with this!"

"Let's hope they like popcorn, too!" Yasmin said.

Just then, Cloe looked out the front glass window and called out. "They're walking away!"

"No, stop them!" said Jade. "We can't let them find Sasha!"

The girls ran to the front doors and began to bang on them to distract the dogs, but they continued to walk away, back in the direction of the toy store.

"We've got to do it now," said Jade. "Pick a dog, girls. On the count of three, open the doors. As soon as the dogs enter, dump your tub on your dog and run out. I'll be right behind!"

"Okay!" said Yasmin.

"Here we go! One . . ." began Jade, ". . . two . . . three!"

Yasmin and Cloe flung open the doors and called to the dogs. The dogs turned back and began charging in the direction of the theater.

"Here they come!" shouted Yasmin.

"Get ready!" shouted Cloe.

Just as the dogs passed over the threshold, Jade gave the word. "Now!" she yelled.

Jade, Cloe, and Yasmin threw their popcorn on top of the dogs. The dogs immediately became disoriented and bumped into one another.

"Now's our chance! Run!" yelled Cloe.

Cloe jumped out, followed by Yasmin and then finally Jade. The dogs quickly turned and charged at the girls. But just as they did, the front doors slammed shut.

"Grab that planter, Cloe!" yelled Yasmin.

The girls quickly maneuvered another planter securely against the theater. The doors were closed. And the dogs were locked inside.

"We did it!" cheered Cloe.

"Now let's find Sasha," Jade said.

Just then, a familiar voice echoed through the mall.

"I'm right here!" said Sasha. The girls looked around, but couldn't see where the voice was coming from. "No, silly! Up here!" The girls looked up to see Sasha nestled on top of a cellular phone kiosk.

"Bunny Boo!" squealed Cloe. "How'd you get up there?"

"I hopped, of course!" Sasha responded. "Now get me down from here!"

The girls reached for their friend and helped her down from her perch.

"I saw what you guys did! Nice job!" said Sasha.

"Thanks, it was Jade's idea!" said Cloe.

"Good job, Kool Kat!" said Sasha. "You saved us all!"

"We did it together," said Jade modestly. "But now, can we please get something to eat?"

"Yeah!" said Cloe.

"I'm starving!" said Yasmin.

The girls made their way back to the food court. Dinner was definitely overdue.

chapter eight

"Well, that was absolutely de-lish!" exclaimed Cloe as she leaned back, stuffed from dinner.

"Who wants dessert?" asked Jade, holding up a plate of cookies she had baked at the local cookie shop.

"None for me," Sasha said as she got up and began to walk around the table. "I think I need to stretch."

"Hey!" said Yasmin. "Would you believe it's nearly eleven?"

"I really wish we could've made the dance," said Cloe.

"Yeah. Me, too," said Yasmin.

The girls began to clear the table.

"So what's next?" asked Sasha.

"Girls? Isn't it obvious?" asked Jade, getting pumped up. The others stared back at her blankly. "We're in a mall? Hello?"

"Yeah, so . . ." responded Yasmin.

"Let's shop!" Jade exclaimed.

Cloe turned to Sasha. "You know, she is right," she said.

"Of course she is!" sang Yasmin. "Let's do it!

The girls quickly cleaned up and headed out into the mall.

"Well, where should we go first?" asked Cloe.

"You know, I've always wanted to hit that really funky goth-looking store Grave Headz," said Jade.

"I'm game!" said Sasha.

"Cool! Let's go!" said Yasmin as the girls took off up the escalator.

Minutes later, the girls were knee-deep in the coolest, cutting-edge fashions. Jade jumped out from behind a wall display decked in a black-and-red striped shirt that was cut off at the waist. Dressed in a blue-black mini, she looked like she was club-cool ready.

"Nice look!" squealed Sasha.

"Yeah, you can make any look awesome!" said Cloe, who was in a green and black velour dress with a satin sparkle throw.

"Well, look at you!" said Yasmin. "You're awesome, too!"

"What about me?" said Sasha as she twirled in a pair of very formfitting stone-washed jeans and white lacy top.

"Superstylin'!" said Yasmin.

"I can live with that!" Sasha replied, laughing.

"I've just got to try these leather pants on," announced Yasmin as she jumped into a nearby dressing room and began to change. "Hey, Cloe, can you get me a size bigger?" she asked. Cloe went back to grab one, but there weren't any available.

"They don't have any more," Cloe said.

"Well, these are too small," said Yasmin sadly.

"C'mon, Princess, show us how they look," said Sasha.

"I look ridiculous!" shouted Yasmin from behind the curtain.

"Come on and show us," said Jade, growing more eager every second.

"I'm embarrassed," said Yasmin.

"Would you just come out here?" demanded Sasha.

"Okay," said Yasmin. "Just don't laugh." Yasmin slowly opened the curtain and stepped out. The girls took one look and burst out laughing. Yasmin definitely needed a bigger size. The hem of her pants rose above her ankles—and not because they were cropped!

"You look like your clothes shrank!" joked Cloe.

"Maybe you could start a new trend!" Jade said.

Yasmin jumped back behind the curtain. "Not funny! I told you I looked ridiculous."

The girls continued to laugh and try on more funky outfits. After practically all of the fashions Grave Headz had to offer had been tried on, they left and headed to their favorite music store, Funk Out!, for some killer tunes. Sasha switched on the sound system and popped in some rockin' new music.

"Oh, check it out, the latest fashion mags!" said Cloe, making her way over to the magazine counter.

"Hey, anybody up for total annihilation?" asked Jade. The girls turned around to find Jade jamming at the local game station. "I know I am gonna make it to the seventh level tonight!"

Sasha and Yasmin rolled their eyes and smiled. They knew there was definitely no way out of the mall *now*.

"Check out this new groove I came up with," said Sasha as she twisted her body and shuffled her feet from side to side to the music blaring overhead.

"Nice one," Yasmin said. "But what about adding a little strut?" Yasmin showed her what she meant and Sasha picked up on the groove. A moment later, both girls were dancing in time to the tunes.

Seeing them both dance, Cloe ran up next to her friends and started dancing with them. "Let me try!" she said as she began to sway from side to side.

"Now this is what I call a dance party!" shouted Yasmin.

"Hey, Jade! Get over here!" said Sasha.

Jade turned to find all three girls grooving it up. Feeling the funk within, she quickly dropped her gaming handset and joined in. "Break it down!" she sang as all the girls danced together. Jade grabbed Cloe and attempted to dip her, but suddenly lost her balance. Both girls fell down on the ground and began laughing.

"This is way fun!" yelled Sasha.

"Hey! Let's hit Strut It!" said Cloe, referring to a cool shoe store that was located just across from the music store. "I've got a need to step out!"

The girls quickly made their way out of the music store.

"I can't wait to try on those new black boots I saw last week," said Sasha.

"Yeah, those were pretty cool," said Jade.

As the girls were walking, Yasmin noticed the bookstore. "Hey, guys, I'm gonna go check out the bookstore."

"What? You don't want to try on shoes?" asked Cloe. "You feeling okay, girl?"

"Of course, but that new mystery just came out, and I haven't checked it out yet!" said Yasmin.

The girls looked at Yasmin. "It's the third in a series," Yasmin said matter-of-factly.

"Okay, cool!" said Jade. "We'll meet you out here in like twenty minutes."

Cloe, Sasha, and Jade raced into Strut It! while Yasmin made her way to the bookstore. As she entered the bookstore, she got a warm feeling inside. *All the books in the world*, she thought. *This is gonna be fun*. Yasmin made her way to the new release section and grabbed a copy of the book she had been waiting all year to read. The cover read *Night Trap*. Yasmin smiled. This was definitely a story she could relate to. Yasmin made her way to the back of the store and took a seat at a large table. She opened the book and began reading.

Meanwhile, across the way, Cloe was checking out her reflection in front of a long mirror. "These definitely make me look much taller," she said.

"Yeah, but they're too clunky," said Sasha.

"No, they're not," responded Cloe.

"Oh, yeah?" said Sasha. "Hey, Jade! You like these shoes or what?"

On the other side of the store, Jade was standing in front of another mirror admiring the new shoes on her feet. "What'd you say?" asked Jade.

"Cloe's shoes? Hot or not?" asked Sasha again.

Jade turned to look at Cloe's feet. "Not!" she said.

"Maybe you're right. They're too . . . blah!" said Cloe.

"I think our job here is done, ladies!" said Sasha.

"Yeah, remember what you like so we can come back tomorrow and pick it up!" said Cloe.

"Come back tomorrow?" asked Sasha. "I think I need a vacation from this place."

"Well, not me!" Jade chimed in. "I could live here!"

Sasha and Cloe looked at Jade and smiled. They knew she meant it. She *really* could live in the mall.

The girls put everything back and made their way out of the store.

"I'll get Yasmin!" said Jade as she ran into the bookstore.

"What time is it now?" asked Cloe.

Sasha looked at her watch. "Getting close to midnight. And bedtime. What is it, Angel?" she asked, seeing Cloe's face fall slightly.

"I was just thinking how different this night would've been if we had gone to the dance," said Cloe.

"I know. It would've been so cool," responded Sasha. "And you should've won that contest. Your design was so smokin'!"

"Thanks, but unfortunately not quite good enough," said Cloe, when suddenly Jade rushed out of the bookstore.

"Sasha! Cloe!" she said with panic in her voice.

"What is it?" responded Cloe.

"Yasmin's gone!" shouted Jade.

Sasha turned to look at Cloe. *Oh, no,* they thought. *Not again.*

chapter nine

"Gone?" exclaimed Cloe.

"Stop playing around!" said Sasha. "She's got to be there."

"No. I'm serious," said Jade. "She's not in there!"

Sasha and the girls made their way into the bookstore.

"Princess?" yelled Sasha. "Where are you?"

But there was no response.

"I'll check in the back," said Cloe as she dashed to the back of the store.

"We were only gone for, like, half an hour!" said Jade. "It doesn't make any sense."

Cloe returned from the back of the store wearing a confused look on her face. "She's not back there."

"Well, then she must've stepped out or something," said Sasha.

Sasha walked out of the store and began scanning the mall. Across the way was a furniture store. Right next to it was a video arcade. "Come on," Sasha said. "Maybe she's playing air hockey or something."

The girls made their way into the arcade with its blinking lights and laser sounds. Again, they called out for Yasmin, but there was no response.

"I don't think she's in here," said Jade over the loud noise.

"Neither do I," said Cloe.

"Well, she couldn't have just disappeared," Sasha reassured them. "She's got to be around someplace."

The girls left the arcade and stood in the empty mall.

"Okay, Cloe, you and Jade go that way," Sasha began. "And I'll go this way."

Cloe gave Jade a look. "I don't think we should split up," she said. "I mean, what happens if we lose each other?"

"Okay. Let's think logically. If you were Yasmin,

where would you go?" asked Jade. The girls thought a moment.

"The shoe store?" responded Sasha.

"The bookstore?" responded Cloe.

"Good suggestions, but we know she is in neither of *those* places," Jade responded as she brushed her bangs away from her eyes.

"So where else?" asked Cloe.

"What about the candy store?" said Sasha.

"Good one, Bunny," responded Jade. "Yasmin can never resist something sweet to eat."

"Let's hit it then!" exclaimed Sasha. The girls walked in the direction of Cool Candy, the candy store everybody loved to stop at when they shopped. They called out several times to Yasmin. But there was no answer.

"This is way weird," said Jade.

The girls reached the candy store and called out to Yasmin. But again, there was no response.

"Where could she be?" asked Cloe.

"Don't worry, Angel," said Sasha. "She couldn't have just disappeared." Sasha reached into a nearby gum ball machine, pulled out a pink gum ball, and handed it to Cloe.

"Thanks, Sasha," said Cloe.

"Let's try someplace else," Jade said as she grabbed a quick handful of licorice before leaving.

"Hey, maybe she stopped at the Stylin' Hair Studio," said Sasha. "She really made a mess of herself with that shake machine back at the food court."

"Yeah, maybe she went to freshen up," said Jade.

The girls made their way back to the Stylin' Hair Studio. When they arrived, it was apparent that nobody had been there since Jade and Sasha's visit earlier that evening.

"It's just how we left it," said Jade.

"Yeah," agreed Sasha. "She hasn't been here."

"Maybe we should just go back to the shoe store," said Cloe.

"Yeah, she's probably there looking for *us*," Jade added.

"You may be right!" said Sasha. "Let's go."

The girls hurried back to the shoe store. As soon as they got there, Jade inspected it while Sasha and Cloe inspected the bookstore. After a few moments, the girls found themselves in the center of the mall again—without Yasmin. Frustrated, the girls sat on a nearby bench.

"This just doesn't add up," said Sasha.

"We should've set up a home base," said Jade. "You know, a place where we could meet if we got lost."

Suddenly, Jade stood up. "I think I found her," she said.

"Where?" asked Cloe, rising to her feet.

"Look!" said Jade as she pointed toward the furniture store they were seated in front of. Across the way, nestled in a plush recliner, sat Yasmin with a book on her lap.

"She's asleep," said Cloe, beaming with relief.

"Let's go wake her," said Jade.

All three girls ran across the mall and into the furniture store. Quietly, they slipped down next to her.

"Yasmin," said Cloe gently.

"It's time to rise and shine," said Jade.

Yasmin slowly opened her eyes and caught a glimpse of her friends all around her. She cleared her throat and whispered to them. "Where am I?" she asked.

"In the mall," said Sasha. "We thought you had gone."

Yasmin looked down and grabbed the book from her lap. "I remember I was checking out this book over in the bookstore, but I couldn't get comfy. So I came over here and got cozy," she said slowly.

"Well, you forgot to tell us that," said Cloe.

"How was the book?" asked Sasha.

"Well, let's just say, it put me to sleep," joked Yasmin. The girls laughed. "What happened to you guys?"

"Funny you should ask," said Cloe. "We were looking for . . ."

". . . Dessert!" interrupted Jade as she handed Yasmin a bright blue piece of licorice.

chapter ten

"We could try the department stores," Jade suggested as she and the girls were walking through the center of the mall, window-shopping for a place to sleep. The night was nearly over, and now the time had come to relax and rest.

"Yeah, or we could go back to that furniture store we found Yasmin in," said Sasha.

"I wouldn't recommend it," responded Yasmin, rubbing the kink out of her neck. The girls turned to her and smiled.

"Well, where then?" asked Yasmin.

"I know the perfect place," said Jade, coming to a halt in the mall.

"Where?" asked Cloe excitedly.

Jade pointed to a store across the way. It was called Roughin' It!, and it was an army surplus store.

"Hey! Of course!" said Cloe.

Sasha and Yasmin looked at each other suspiciously. "Are you sure you wouldn't want to spend the night in a more comfy place?" asked Yasmin.

"What are you saying?" said Jade. "We can pretend we're camping in the woods!"

"I gotcha, Jade!" said Cloe. "Hey, girls, it'll be fun."

"Yeah, I guess so," said Yasmin.

"Okay, let's go look," said Sasha.

The girls walked into the store to check out the accommodations. Inside, tents were set up and super-snuggly sleeping bags were unfolded. One cool display created the atmosphere of a real camping trip with a fake campfire and scenic woodland backdrop.

"This is so awesome," said Yasmin, now a believer.

"Yeah, I can hang, too," said Sasha. "Let's do it!"

The girls grabbed the thickest sleeping bags from the shelf and set them out in front of the fake fire.

"What a night," said Yasmin.

"It's been a crazy one," Jade said.

As the girls continued to set up, a lull came over the group.

"Everybody okay?" asked Sasha.

"Not . . . quite," Cloe admitted quietly.

"What is it?" Sasha asked, concerned.

"I guess it's just that the night is coming to a close," said Yasmin.

"Yeah, and . . . ?" responded Sasha.

"And despite the fact that it's been totally fun," started Jade, "we still missed the Homecoming dance."

"Yeah, and we were waiting for it for so long," Cloe said. "It was the party of the year. Now we're going to have to hear all about it on Monday from Cameron and Dylan and the rest of the gang."

"Talking about all the cool music they played. All the yummy food they served," said Yasmin.

"All the far-out outfits everybody was wearing," added Jade.

"We'll only get to see it in pictures," said Cloe, thinking back once again to her loss in the *Picture Perfect!* contest.

"But we had an even better time here!" reminded Sasha.

The girls smiled and then turned away.

"Believe me, I feel awful about it, too," said Sasha. "But what can we do? We're stuck here!"

Suddenly, Jade jumped up. "I've got an idea!" she exclaimed. "Why don't we recreate the Homecoming dance right here?"

The girls turned to one another, confused.

"How?" asked Cloe.

"It's simple. We have everything right here!" responded Jade. "We have the music. We have the food. We even have the space! Let's make it a dance to end all dances!"

"That's a great idea!" said Cloe. "We can make it even better than Homecoming!"

Yasmin and Sasha looked at each other and smiled. "What do you say, Bunny?" asked Yasmin.

"Let's do it, Princess! This is gonna be off-the-hook!" said Sasha, jumping up.

"Okay, I've got the sweets and desserts," announced Yasmin.

"I've got the tunes!" said Sasha.

"But who's gonna help me decorate the place?" asked Jade. The girls turned to Cloe, knowing she was the one for the job.

"Well, if you don't mind a runner-up helping you," began Cloe, "then I guess I'll do it."

"Great!" shouted Jade. "Let's hit it!"

The girls ran out of the store in the direction of the mall center. There was no time to waste. The party wasn't quite over yet.

■ ■ ■ ■

Jade and Cloe hit the party favor store, Party Palace, first. They grabbed tons of multi-colored streamers, napkins, and hanging lights.

"Grab a posterboard, too!" said Cloe.

"What for?" asked Jade.

"You'll see," responded Cloe, smiling, as she made her way out of the store.

Meanwhile, Sasha jetted back to Funk Out! and grabbed a couple of groovy dance CDs she had listened to earlier. As she was making her way out of the store, she realized the obvious: What was she going to play the CDs on? She didn't have a boom box and singing was definitely out of the question. But then the answer came to her: she could stop by the local electronics store and borrow a boom box. They always had tons of display models to play with. Quickly, she made her way there, before returning back to the girls.

Yasmin stopped by Cool Candy first and then to her favorite bakery shop, Chocolate Delight. From dark chocolate peanut clusters and candy truffles to scrumptious cupcakes and cookies, she grabbed a little bit of everything to make sure all of the girls had something to snack on.

In practically no time, the girls met in the mall center and raced to set things up. Yasmin began by placing all of the sweets into bowls that she'd borrowed from the home décor section of the local department store. Sasha plugged in the boom box and set it on a nearby bench that was decorated with shimmering streamers by Jade.

Cloe hung colorful party lights from the floor above to give the place that dance-floor funk feel. As she did, she caught a glimpse of the Fashion Friendz-y! store window across the way that she had seen earlier, the one with the boring store display. Cloe smiled. She knew just what to do.

"Well, I think this party is finally ready to begin!" yelled Sasha over the music.

The girls turned to see the incredible transformation that had taken place. What was once just a space connecting the wings of the mall was now the coolest high school dance party ever! From spinning lights and hanging decorations to rockin' tunes and loads and loads of delectable treats, it was a Homecoming dance like no other.

"Looks awesome!" said Yasmin. "Who wants a tasty treat?"

"I do," responded the other girls at the same time as they made their way over and grabbed some bits of candy and chocolate.

"You know, girls, I hate to break it to ya, but something is definitely missing," said Jade with a grin on her face.

"What?" said Sasha in disbelief.

"Boys!" responded Jade. "We need a little male energy, don'tcha think?"

"Well, sure. But next to us getting out of here, I think that's impossible!" responded Yasmin.

"Oh, no, it's not," replied Jade as she made her way over to a nearby store window and grabbed a male mannequin. "Ladies, meet my date for the evening!"

The girls broke out into laughter.

"Hey, that's not a bad idea," said Cloe as she raced over to the store and grabbed a mannequin for herself. "What do you think, Jade? Is he my type?"

"Totally!" said Jade, cracking up.

Yasmin and Sasha ran over to another store window and grabbed dates for themselves. "What do you think, Yas?" asked Sasha.

"You know how I like them strong and silent," joked Yasmin. "He's a keeper."

"Oh and your guy rocks! I just love his, um, painted blue eyes," said Sasha.

"Thanks, Bunny," said Yasmin. "He appreciates you saying that!"

The girls laughed as they dragged their guys out and placed them in the middle of the floor. With the strobe lights blinking rapidly, they looked almost real.

"So, let's get this party started!" yelled Sasha.

"No, not yet!" responded Jade.

"What is it *now*, Jade?" replied Yasmin.

"Well, I don't know about you, but when I *go* out, I like to get *decked* out!" said Jade.

Sasha smiled. How could they forget to dress for the party?

"You're right, Jade!" Yasmin said. "We need to look our best!"

"Let's hit it, girls!" squealed Cloe.

The girls raced back to their favorite clothing store, Chix, and grabbed the funky fashion items they had been wearing when the lights went out. Back in the dressing room, it was time to dress up all over again.

"Does this look familiar?" asked Cloe as she stepped out of the dressing room. Decked in the same red and gold summer dress, Cloe now topped the outfit off with a pair of gorgeous platform Mary Jane shoes and a sparkling gold necklace that made her look classy *and* wild.

"The boys are gonna love you in that!" joked

Yasmin as she sauntered out in the same spectacular Victorian blouse she had worn before, but instead of the familiar woven-gray satin skirt, she now wore a pair of vintage-looking denim jeans.

"Cool combo!" said Sasha. "But check *me* out." The girls turned to find Sasha spinning in front of the dressing room mirror in a baby-blue skirt and gray halter that was accented by a pair of knee-high blue and black boots.

"Wow, nice!" responded Cloe. "What about that other outfit?"

"I think this fits my mood a little better now," responded Sasha.

"Jade?" said Yasmin. "You ready?"

"I'm not sure which outfit to wear," replied Jade.

"Oh, here we go again!" said Yasmin.

"Just kidding," said Jade as she sashayed out in an elegant gem-studded peach dress, white stockings, and white shoes.

"Look at you!" said Sasha. "You look exquisite!"

"Thank you!" said Jade. "All I need is a subtle hint of rose make-up and I'm all set."

"Oh, that's right!" exclaimed Yasmin. "We mustn't forget that."

"Let's go!" said Sasha.

The girls made their way to Kiss 'N' Make-up on the other side of the mall. As soon as they got there, Sasha hit the lip gloss, Yasmin hit the perfume, Jade hit the blush, and Cloe hit the mascara.

"What do you think?" asked Jade, wearing a subtle touch of pink blush.

"Excellent," said Yasmin, who had already sprayed a touch of her favorite perfume and was now applying eyeliner to her beautiful brown eyes.

"How do I look?" asked Sasha, referring to the violet lip gloss she had just put on.

"Nice!" said Jade.

"Cloe, what do you think?" asked Yasmin as she turned to show Cloe her look and found Cloe gone. "Hey, where's Cloe?"

"That's it!" said Sasha. "Everybody's getting leashes to wear!"

"Well, she was just here a minute ago!" said

Yasmin. "She couldn't have gotten far!" The girls ran out of the store and scanned the mall.

"Cloe! Cloe!" yelled Sasha.

"I'm over here," Cloe yelled back.

"Where is here?" asked Jade.

"Over here!" repeated Cloe. "What da ya think?" she asked.

The girls turned and saw Cloe, beaming from ear to ear. She was sitting in the front window of the clothing store Fashion Friendz-y!, which was now decorated to look like a fashion runway, complete with beaming spotlights, a fake crowd, and a glittering catwalk. On a big banner above hung a sign that read *The Homecoming Collection*. "Do you like?" she asked.

"Awesome!" said Jade.

"When did you have time to do all this?" asked Yasmin.

"Let's just say, 'fast' is my middle name," Cloe responded. "That, and you guys take quite a long time to decide on make-up!" The girls laughed.

"This is even better than your *Picture Perfect!*

entry!" exclaimed Sasha.

"Yeah, too bad the students at Stiles High can't see this now!" said Yasmin. "You've really outdone yourself, Cloe."

"Thanks! But students or no students, *I* like it," said Cloe.

"And that's all that matters," added Jade.

"Exactly," said Cloe. "Anyway, I figured we needed to take pictures to mark the occasion. So naturally, we needed a backdrop to go with it!"

"I hate to burst your bubble, Angel," said Sasha, "but we don't have a camera."

"Oh, yes, we do!" said Cloe. "How could you forget that Yasmin's phone has a built-in camera?"

"I forgot, too!" blurted Yasmin as she pulled it out.

"Well, let's snap some pics!" said Jade. The girls ran over to the display and stood atop the catwalk. "Okay, you three go first and then we can switch off," said Jade.

"We don't have to," said Yasmin. "My camera has a timer, too! That I *do* remember!"

"Cool!" said Cloe.

"I'm just not sure how it works," Yasmin said, fiddling with the camera. Suddenly, an hourglass appeared in the display followed by a timer countdown. "I did it! Quick, get in line." Yasmin perched the camera on a nearby bench, and jumped in front of the runway back-drop.

"Okay, girls, be beautiful!" exclaimed Cloe. The girls struck a pose as the flash went off.

"Let's take another one!" said Sasha. Yasmin ran back to the camera and hit the button again. And again. And again. This was a moment to remember forever.

As soon as the pictures were all taken, the girls headed back to the mall center. It was time to officially celebrate the Stiles High Homecoming. Once they got there, Sasha turned up the music and the girls began to dance.

"What a party!" yelled Cloe over the music. "I can't believe how much fun I'm having!"

"This evening turned out alright after all!" said Yasmin.

"Sure did, and you know why?" asked Jade.

"Because we have each other," said Sasha.

"Right on!" said Cloe.

The girls danced nearly all night, stopping to take a break here and there for a quickie goodie before jamming it up all over again. It was without a doubt the coolest night of the year and everything the girls could have wanted it to be.

chapter eleven

For nearly three hours, the girls laughed and danced and had the time of their lives at their impromptu Homecoming gala. Soon after, the girls cleaned everything up and put everything back where it belonged. The mannequins went back into the store windows. The lights and streamers were returned to the party store. The stylin' fashions went back to Chix and to the other fashion stores from which they were borrowed. The food court was cleaned. Even the dogs that were trapped in the movie theater were checked on to make sure they were okay—which they were. Now it was time to get some well-needed rest. The girls washed themselves up at the local hair salon and found themselves at the final stop on their all-night shopping extravaganza, the camping store.

"Well, this isn't exactly what I had in mind for my big sleepover," Yasmin began, "but what a party!"

"Man, I'm beat," said Sasha as she rolled out her sleeping bag.

"Wait, we can't go to sleep yet!" said Jade. "We need to figure out how we're gonna get out of here!"

"Jade's right," said Cloe. "We need to have a plan. If we don't, they may catch us and think we broke in or something."

"Good point, Jade," said Sasha as she sat up and turned to Jade. "You know, I gotta tell you, that thing Mr. Kelly said to you, about not working well under pressure and being a leader and all that, well, he's all wrong. I mean, take tonight, for example. If it wasn't for you finding the lever, we'd still probably be stuck in Chix."

"Yeah," Yasmin chimed in. "And you were so quick-thinking when it came to trapping those dogs."

"And it was your idea to have our own Homecoming dance right here!" said Cloe. "That was so cool!"

Jade smiled and began to blush. "Thanks, guys. It means a lot to hear that."

"Kool Kat, on Monday, I'm telling Mr. Kelly that I want us to split responsibilities for the yearbook. This year,

Stiles High is gonna have two yearbook presidents."

"You mean it?" asked Jade.

"Of course I do," responded Sasha.

Jade reached over and hugged Sasha. "Thanks," she said.

"Well, now that that's settled, how are we gonna get out of here?" asked Cloe.

"The mall opens at eight in the morning," said Yasmin. "So the workers must start getting here at least a half an hour before that, right?"

"Right. So we gotta be outta here by seven-thirty," said Jade.

"We have to be extremely careful not to be seen," said Sasha.

"It's so funny, last night all we wanted to do was be seen so we could get out of here and now it's the other way around," said Cloe.

"Jade, set the alarm on your watch to ring at seven," said Yasmin.

"Well, good night, ladies," said Cloe as she snuggled in her cozy-comfy sleeping bag.

"Pleasant dreams," said Yasmin.

"Thanks for a great night," said Sasha.

"It's one I'll never forget," added Jade.

The girls turned off the electric lantern that illuminated the room and slowly drifted off to sleep.

■ ■ ■ ■

"Wake up," whispered Yasmin to the other girls who were still sleeping. "It's nearly eight already."

Sasha sprang up and rubbed her eyes. "Eight?" she said.

"Yeah, we overslept," said Yasmin.

"Cloe, we're late," said Sasha.

"Oh, just five more minutes," said Cloe as she rolled over and let out a big sigh.

"The mall opens in twenty minutes," replied Sasha.

"What?" said Cloe, waking up and rising to her feet.

"Jade," said Yasmin, "it's time to get up."

Jade opened her eyes and checked her watch. "We're totally late!" she shouted.

The girls put away their sleeping bags and quickly

made their way to the front of the store. As they did, two shopkeepers were setting things up.

"Yeah, they say somebody broke in last night," said one of the shopkeepers to the other. "The funny thing is, nothing was taken."

The girls looked at one another.

"We gotta get out of here, like now," whispered Jade.

As the shopkeepers turned their backs, the girls quietly made their way out of the store and quickly raced to the front of the mall. Already, the mall muzak had begun.

"Stay low," said Cloe. "We're nearly there."

"What time is it now?" asked Sasha.

"We've got fifteen minutes," responded Jade.

The girls turned a bend and were only yards away from the huge front doors in the center of the mall, when they suddenly stopped dead in their tracks; because standing there on the other side of the doors was a huge group of people waiting anxiously to come in!

"Oh, no!" shouted Jade.

"It's the early-bird shoppers!" said Sasha. "Retreat!"

The girls ran back behind a nearby planter.

"How are we going to get out if they're there?" asked Yasmin.

"We'll have to exit through another entrance," said Cloe.

"Yeah, we can get out through the side door over by Cool Candy," said Jade.

The girls ran across the mall to the side entrance doorway. When they got there, there were no shoppers in sight. "Let's do it," said Sasha as she reached for the door. "It's locked!" she said. "Jade, what time do you have?"

"Just over ten minutes before the mall opens," Jade replied.

"Let's just hope that the doors automatically open at eight," said Cloe.

The girls hid behind a nearby trash receptacle, waiting for eight to come. Every second seemed to last an eternity. They knew they were close, but they weren't out of the woods yet. Suddenly, they spotted a security guard who was walking in the direction of the doors. The girls quickly jumped back.

"Did he see us?" said Cloe, her voice shaking.

"I don't think so," said Yasmin.

The security guard approached the doors and pulled out a key.

"He's opening it," said Sasha.

"Okay, look, guys. When he walks away, we gotta make a break for it," said Jade.

"Yeah, and be quick," said Yasmin.

The security guard swung the door open, peered out, and then closed it again before slowly walking away in the other direction.

"Okay, now's our chance!" whispered Jade. "Let's go."

The girls ran to the door and reached out to open it, when suddenly a deep voice echoed from behind them. "Hey, you girls!" said the voice. The girls slowly turned around to find the security guard standing behind them. The girls looked at one another. They knew the jig was up. It was time to come clean.

"Look, officer, we didn't mean to be here," began Cloe. "It was an honest mistake."

"You have to believe us! We didn't break any laws!" said Jade.

The security guard looked at them suspiciously. "I know what's going on."

The girls stopped talking. "You do?" responded Jade.

"I see it every year about this time," said the security guard. The girls looked at one another. This was it. Welcome to a life behind bars. "Today is the start of our huge Fall Sales event, and you girls wanted to get a head start on shopping before everybody else."

"Umm . . . well . . ." Sasha responded.

"Look, I understand," said the security guard. "I have a daughter about your age and she's the same way."

"You do?" asked Yasmin.

"Yeah. Okay, I'll tell you what I'm gonna do," said the security guard. "The mall doesn't officially open for another ten minutes, but a lot of these stores are already open. So . . . go ahead."

"Go ahead?" asked Sasha.

"Yeah," said the security guard. "Go get a head start. I won't stop you."

"Oh, well, we wouldn't want to impose," said Yasmin.

"No, it's my pleasure," said the security guard.

"But, well, it really isn't fair to the rest of the early shoppers," said Cloe.

"No, I insist," the security guard said as he shuffled the girls back into the mall. "Go get whatever it is you came here for. Consider it . . . a gift."

The girls looked at one another and gave a low sigh. It was no use. There was no way of getting out of this. They were stuck in the mall all over again.

"Well, thank you, sir," said Yasmin.

"Yes, thank you," said Sasha humbly.

The girls walked away and began to giggle. They would have to wait just a little while longer before they would be able to leave the mall.

"Well, here we go again," said Yasmin.

"Now, did I hear wrong, or did he say Fall Sales event?" asked Jade.

"Yep, that's what he said," responded Cloe. "He also said that we have a head start over everybody else." The girls stopped and looked at one another.

"Who are we kidding?" said Sasha.

"Yeah! Let's hit it!" shouted Yasmin.

The girls quickly ran up the escalator. The after-party was just beginning.